J
HER

Hermes, Patricia

Wild year : Joshua's Oregon Trail
diary, book three

The Wild Year

Joshua's Oregon Trail Diary

· Book Three ·

by Patricia Hermes

Scholastic Inc. New York

Willamette Valley, Oregon
1849

April 15, 1849

Not yet dawn. But I'm up and dressed. Dressed means shoes and pants. I have my notebook and pencil and I've climbed the hill beside the house. The trees and orchard are just shadows in the mist. The only ones on the hill are me and a big cat, looks like a panther. It slunk off into the trees when it saw me. Maybe it knows there's a bounty on its head — head with the ears attached. I can't sleep none, for some reason. I think it's 'cause spring is coming. Spring always does something to your insides. Makes you want to cut loose. Makes me want to get on Hurricane, my horse, and just fly over the hills.

Ma would kill me.

She thinks I'm getting like Pa — always listening to the call of the wild.

Right now, the call is from Ma. Wanting me to milk Laurie, our cow.

More later.

Later

Ma wants to know why I'm out walking around half naked. She says I'll catch my death of cold.

I just say, "Yes, Ma." There's no sense arguing. Ma's convinced I'm going to die. At least once a day she says I'm going to *catch my death* from something or other. You'd think that with all we've been through, she'd know I'm made of strong stuff. But I guess it's because she's a ma. Pa says it's the job of a woman to worry.

April 16

I need to tell about this diary. Grampa said not everybody does what we did, crossing from Missouri to Oregon on that long, lonesome trail. He wanted me to record it. He said, "Tell it all — the good and the not-so-good."

Soon, I will be ten years old, almost a man. So I will make a list of all the things I did when I was nine. Just this past year.

Nighttime

Here is my list:

Left our home in St. Joseph, Missouri, to come to Oregon. I came with Grampa, Ma and Pa, and my little sister, Becky. Ma's twin sister, Aunt Lizzie, and her husband, Uncle Arthur, and my cousins Charlie and Rachel came, too, in their own wagon. (Charlie's not just my cousin. He's my best friend.)

We went thousands of miles across the prairie. It poured down rain. The sun baked us like muffins in an oven. Dust choked us. We crossed rivers that tried to pull us down and drown us. We took our wagons apart to haul them up mountains. Sometimes, the wagons broke loose, and people got run over and died. Other people died from cholera. We buried them right on the trail.

Rachel, my baby cousin, got hung by the sash of her nightdress. And she died.

I got lost. And I could have died.

I killed a buffalo!

I saw Indians. I was scared at first. But I'm not scared of them any more.

I saved Becky from drowning when she fell in the river.

Aunt Lizzie got a new baby.

I got a new baby brother.

I got a new horse.

I like my horse better.

I guess Baby Hector will be all right, if he can ever stop squalling.

April 17

Grampa was my friend, but he was still lonesome. Grandma died before I even got born. He met Miss Emmaline on the trail and they married. She's young, even younger than Ma. But then, after we were already in Oregon, Grampa got killed helping the Hull family in the big flood. He got trapped under the wagon and drowned. I never knew I could miss anyone like I miss him.

Miss Emmaline misses him, too. She lives with us now. We try to cheer her up. She's family now.

April 18

Now that we're here in the Willamette Valley, at the end of the trail, we've staked out an entire square mile for our homestead. We cleared the land and planted a garden and an orchard. We built a house and both of our families live in it together. The house started out small. But we are adding on to it. Now, it's long and sprawls all over the top of the hillside. In the middle is a big room, kind of a kitchen and parlor together. On the sides are rooms for sleeping, one side for us, one side for Aunt Lizzie's family. Most times, we all get along real well.

Sometimes, not.

Later

Like now. I hear Ma fussing at Charlie. Seems he tracked in mud all over her clean floor. Ever since we left the trail, Ma cares more about "clean" than about most anything else. Can't say I blame her. I didn't have one bath the whole six months, 'cept for washing in the rivers at times. And sometimes, the river washing wasn't even done on purpose — like when the wagons got turned over and we all got dunked.

April 19

Now that we're here, Pa works all day on our homestead. But at night, he stays up late, reading and talking politics with Uncle Arthur. Pa is very smart. Grampa thought he was too smart. *Too much education and book learning and not enough common sense* — that's what Grampa used to say.

Back in St. Joseph, Pa read a lot but he didn't care about politics and law and such. But when I said that to Pa once, he said, "Josh, Missouri already had laws. Out here, who's going to make laws if we don't?"

I guess I had never thought of that.

April 20

I can tell Pa wants to be part of the new territorial government. He talks about it all the time. And Ma wants no part of it. Last night when Pa was talking, she threw her hands up over her head and walked right out the back door into the night.

More later. Ma wants me to watch Becky so she won't wander away.

Later

Ma and Aunt Lizzie and the two babies, Hector and Isabel, are going to visit Mrs. Hull. Miss Emmaline is going, too. Mr. Hull got killed by a falling tree right after we came here. Now, Ma and the other women take turns visiting and bringing food to Mrs. Hull. Miss Emmaline goes to do repairs and such. Miss Emmaline is so delicate looking, but she can handle a hammer and nails as good as a man.

Later. Still with Becky.

It's taking Ma a long time. I get so tired of Becky. She just asked me to sing "Yankee Doodle" for her. When I got to the part about "Stuck a feather in his cap" — I got a long pine needle and stuck it in her hair. It made her giggle.

Now she wants me to do it again.

Won't Ma ever get home?

Later still

Still with Becky. Now she's begging me to take her into the woods. She always wants to go there. That's because Charlie and me tell about the wild animals there. Becky wants to see a bear. But a baby child like Becky can't go in the woods. It's too easy to get lost. Charlie and I even got lost once. She also asked for hide-and-seek. But you can't play that game with Becky because she only hides her head. Then she cries when you find her so easy. So I agreed to play house.

Imagine.

I'm supposed to be the baby and she'll be the mother. I said all right, but I'd have to take a nap. Because that's what babies do. (And because I'm so bored of playing with her.) But then, every two seconds she's poking me, asking if I'm asleep yet.

I gave up trying to nap. I told her we could play school instead. Now I'm being the teacher and writing in my book here. But I have to let her write, too.

That's why the scribbles are here.

$$A \& \text{vn}$$

(That's Becky.)

Still later. At last!

Ma and Miss Emmaline are back home. Becky's decided to pester Ma instead of me. I'm heading for the river. Charlie's down there, fishing.

Evening

We caught ten fish. We kept only three for ourselves — three of the biggest trout I've ever seen. We cleaned them and brought them home for supper. There are so many fish in these rivers, you could almost scoop them out with your bare hands. I've tried, but I can never hold on to them. I've seen bears do it, though. I guess they can hold on because they have claws.

April 21

Yesterday late, Frederick Hull came on down to the river. He's so changed now. Not mean and smart-mouthed. But he makes me sad. We gave him the extra fish we didn't need. His family needs them. With ten children to feed and no pa in the house, it must be real hard.

I wish sometimes I hadn't been so mean to him back on the trail.

It was awfully hard to lose my grampa. Imagine what it's like, losing your very own pa.

April 22

Everyone's talking about the orphan children who have arrived in Oregon City. They lost their parents in the massacre at the Whitman Mission.

The Whitmans were good folks. They had a mission on the Oregon Trail to care for the Indian people and others. But there was an outbreak of measles. Many Indians died. The Indian people thought it was the fault of Dr. Whitman and they attacked the Mission.

They killed the men and women, too. The children hid. The killing went on for three whole days. I can't imagine hiding for three days while your parents got killed!

Now a lady in Oregon City is starting an orphanage and school for the children. Some of the children are being adopted out.

April 23

On the trail, we had a little community, sort of like a neighborhood. One of the families was the Meaneys. Mrs. Meaney was just like her name — mean through and through. Though since we got here, she's been nicer. Now we hear that Mrs. Meaney is planning to adopt an orphan. Everyone wonders if she has really gotten that kindhearted or if there's another reason.

I think there's another reason.

April 24

Mr. Meaney has gone to Oregon City. He's to bring back an orphan by nightfall.

Later

I heard Ma ask Aunt Lizzie why Mrs. Meaney would take an orphan. "Has she really become kindhearted, you think?" Ma asked.

Aunt Lizzie hoisted Baby Isabel on her hip. She wrinkled up her nose. "Kindhearted?" she said. "Nothing of the sort. That woman is looking for a girl to wait on her hand and foot. Just like everyone waited on her on the trail."

Then Aunt Lizzie saw that I was listening. "Never mind me," she said. "I'm just being a bit mean-spirited today." And she sent me away to get a diaper for Isabel.

I went. But I didn't think it was mean-spirited. I think it was the truth.

Evening

Sad today.

Ma and Aunt Lizzie were cooking up a mess of collards and beans for dinner, talking away about this and that recipe. They both love to cook and bake. Miss Emmaline wasn't saying much. But she was trying to help. She's not really much of a cook, though. She's much better at building things and repairing wagon wheels, the kinds of things men do usually. We had just sat down to eat when she remembered she'd put cornbread in the oven. She jumped up and yanked the pan out. But it was all smoking and black. She just busted out in tears. Then she went and tossed the burning bread, pan and all, out the back door.

At first, we all just got real quiet. Even Becky stopped whining. Then Ma got up and went to Miss Emmaline, who was standing there shaking in the doorway. Ma put her arms around her. They stood together for a long time. I think Ma knew that it wasn't the cornbread. It was her missing Grampa so bad. Ma misses him, too, I know.

We all do.

Morning, April 25

Mr. Meaney is back from Oregon City. But without an orphan child. He said that there were none old enough to bother with.

Old enough? Isn't it the little ones who need parents the most?

I saw Ma and Aunt Lizzie exchange looks. I know what they were thinking, 'cause I was thinking it, too. Same thing we all thought yesterday.

Miss Emmaline just looked real thoughtful.

April 26

I heard Ma talk to Pa about the orphans. She didn't exactly say we should take one in. But I did hear her say it would be nice for Becky to have a sister!

Pa didn't say anything. He just looked at Ma, smiling.

They didn't ask my opinion.

Later though, I told Charlie my opinion. I said I think we have enough whiny little girls around here already.

Ma overheard. She said I am the most contrary boy God ever made, and I should be ashamed of myself.

I guess I am. Ashamed of myself, I mean.

But it's still true, what I said. Won't Becky ever stop whining? Even the babies, Isabel and Hector, aren't as much of a bother as she is.

April 27

I asked Ma tonight if I could move my bed into the storeroom out back. It's like a lean-to, open to the stars. I've only asked her about a thousand times. Each time, she says, *We'll see.* That usually means no. I tell her I'm too big to be sharing a room with her and Pa and Becky and Hector. But the real reason is because it makes me restless, being closed up inside a house at night.

I think I'll ask Pa.

April 28

Pa said yes! He helped me move my bed outside to the lean-to. Miss Emmaline helped, too. She even nailed up a shelf next to my bed for my candle and my diary.

My room is not exactly outside. There's a roof and a big shutter to close down over the open side when it rains. Tonight will be my first night out there.

Nighttime

In my new outside room, there's a candle on my shelf lighting my diary. The moon shines in so bright, and the sky is filled with stars.

To think: In St. Joseph, I couldn't wait to sleep out under the stars. Then, after six months on the trail, I couldn't wait to sleep in a bed inside a house. And now I have a bed. And I have a house. And all I want to do is sleep out under the stars again.

Makes me wonder about myself. Is it just that I'm growing and changing? Or am I really contrariwise? Maybe Ma's right. Maybe I am just the most contrary boy God ever made.

April 29

Ma says I'm getting mouthy. Pa's almost always having to make peace between Ma and me. I don't mean to get Ma riled up. I just can't do anything right with her these days. Like last night, she came to the lean-to to make me blow out my candle and put away my diary. She said I would burn the house down, with the candle so low. I told her, "But I have to write in my diary. I promised Grampa."

She said I'd better promise myself to stop being so mouthy.

I'm promising myself to try harder.

April 30

Maybe being almost ten is what's making me restless. Least, that's what Pa says. I just know I can't stand staying put all day. And I can't stand being holed up inside a house at night. I wish I could be a trapper. I see those Frenchmen in the woods. I love to follow them, see what they're up to. Yesterday, I sneaked after one man. He was huge and all grizzled and dirty looking. But he moved through those woods so quiet-like, you'd think he was a shadow. I guess I wasn't as quiet as him, though I tried to be. Because after a bit, he stopped and turned to me. He shook his head a little, as if to say, *Quiet!* But he smiled at me all the same. Then he turned and went on. Maybe come winter, I could go off to Canada with the trappers. But only if I had some pelts of my own to sell or trade. Then I could bring back money for Ma and Pa. Show them what I could do on my own.

They'd never let me go.

May 1
A new month

Another thought: Maybe what I should do is get on Hurricane and ride off to the California gold mines. Before Grampa died, I said that to him once. He said that only a fool risks his life for gold.

But I wouldn't be risking my life. Lots of folks have gone. And they haven't come back dead. Then, when I found gold — they say it's just laying around in the streams, for you to scoop up — I could bring it back here. Ma and Pa would be rich.

Morning, May 2

I talked to Frederick Hull. I asked him if he still thought about going to California. He was going to go once before. He said no. His folks need him here. He's the pa now in that family.

Imagine being a pa when you're only ten years old.

May 3
Raining

Today, Charlie saw me with this diary. He teases me about it sometimes. One time, he said writing is for girls. Another time, he said I act like I'm a schoolmaster. Today, he asked if I thought I was a *senator*. Miss Emmaline heard and told him to stop teasing. Miss Emmaline always takes up for me. We've gotten to be kind of close. I think maybe it's because of Grampa — both of us missing him so much.

I wonder sometimes if Charlie's jealous because Grampa didn't give him a diary. But other times, I think it's just because he doesn't care for books and writing like I do.

Me, I can't get enough of reading and writing! I have a book of poems that Grampa used to read to Miss Emmaline. They're a bit mushy sounding, but nice.

May 4
Still raining

If I can't go to California or Canada, I want to go to school! Really. I'm missing all the book learning we did back in St. Joseph, Missouri.

I heard there's a school for children in Oregon City. I could ride Hurricane there every day. It takes an hour or more. But I could do it. And that would be adventure enough!

Ma would be too scared to let me go.

May 5
Pouring down rain

Seems like we should all be happy now that we're here and settled. But lately, everybody's every which way with everybody else. Ma is grumpy. Pa has stopped humming. Miss Emmaline wipes away tears when she thinks no one is looking. Becky whines and pulls on Ma. Hector squalls day and night. And Aunt Lizzie frowns so hard some days, her forehead is as rutted looking as the trail bed.

Even Charlie snapped at me today. All I did was ask for a turn with his gun.

I think it's the rain that's making everyone cranky. Seems all it does is rain in Oregon.

May 6

Still raining. One whole week now. Ma is more like a bear than ever. Aunt Lizzie isn't much better. She almost bit my head off earlier. All I did was ask what's for supper. She said, "Have you caught a fish, a squirrel, skinned a rabbit, dug any roots? Done anything useful today? You even forgot to milk Laurie!"

I must've looked surprised, maybe hurt some, because Pa took me aside. He put a hand on my shoulder. He said not to fret. The sun will shine again. And then the women won't be snappish any longer.

I surely hope he's right.

At least Pa's my friend. He and I have always been friends. But seems we're even better friends now in Oregon. I think Pa knows how much I miss Grampa.

Nighttime

Tonight, at supper, Pa and Uncle Arthur were talking about Dr. John McLoughlin. Dr. McLoughlin is an important man in Oregon City. I've not met him. But Pa met him after the flood and they got to be friends. (Actually, I think Dr. McLoughlin lent Pa money to get us started here. But I know Ma doesn't know about that.) Seems Dr. McLoughlin likes to help us settlers. He's going to introduce Pa to some men in the government. I could tell Pa and Uncle Arthur's talk was making Ma unhappy. Her face got even tighter looking than it's been for the past week. And her eyes got all squinchy.

Next day
And still raining

More talk at supper about the new territorial government. Suddenly, Ma burst out, "Why not leave well enough alone? Haven't we caused ourselves enough trouble for a while?"

I could see that took Pa aback some. He didn't say nothing, though.

I wonder why Ma said what she said. How can working for the territorial government be "trouble"?

Morning, May 8

Ma still has that squinchy-eyed look with Pa. She looks just like she looked back in St. Joseph when Pa talked about coming west. So now I have a new thought. Maybe it's not the work with the government that worries Ma, maybe it's gold fever. I know that some people who came on the trail with us have moved on. The whole Drucker family went. They've gone to California, looking for gold. Is Pa thinking of moving on again? Is that what's worrying Ma? Is Dr. McLoughlin going to lend Pa money for a journey again?

Do I dare ask Pa?

Later

I did. Asked him right out, but out of earshot of Ma. He put his hand on my shoulder, like he does sometimes. He said, "No, son. We're here to stay."

That comforted me. Some. 'Cause I surely don't want us all to move on. I don't care if I never see a wagon again in my whole, entire life. But I wouldn't mind going off on my own.

May 9

Listen to this! Tonight, we sat on the porch, Miss Emmaline and me, just the two of us, reading. Suddenly, she looked up and asked if I could keep a secret. Of course I said yes. Her secret? She wants her own house. And she wants to build it herself! She asked if Ma and Aunt Lizzie would feel hurt if she left us.

I was so surprised, I almost fell off the porch. "Aren't you happy here?" I asked.

She says she's happy enough. But she needs her own house. And then she told me the rest of the secret. And that made me almost fall off the porch a second time. She's going to adopt some orphans as soon as her house is built! She made me cross my heart and promise not to tell till she's ready to tell.

I promised. I even said I'd help her to build. And I will.

But I think I will burst with the secret.

Later

Tonight Pa was up late, reading by candlelight. I couldn't sleep none, what with thinking about Miss Emmaline. So after a while, I got up and went out to the kitchen.

Pa looked up and smiled at me. He said he was making notes about the kinds of laws that are needed here in this new territory. Pa went back to his reading then. But first he patted a chair beside him so I could read, too.

I tried, but didn't understand anything in his book. So instead, I went and got Grampa's poetry book and this diary. I sat at the table beside Pa. For a long while, the two of us sat reading and writing together.

It was a real nice feeling.

May 10

Today Charlie and I went out in the woods. Ma wanted me to fill a sack with pine needles so she can stuff pillows. Pa has marked off how far we're allowed to go. He says we need boundaries because it's easy to get lost. And because there are bears and lynxes and wolves. Mostly, the critters don't bother you. But you don't want to get caught downwind of a she-bear with cubs.

Charlie and I stalk the animals sometimes. We follow their feeding trails and water trail down to the river. Today we saw deer and a lynx and two wolves, all drinking together.

Funny how animals can be enemies and still do things together. I wonder if they make a truce ahead of time.

We were hunting, looking for some fresh game for supper. Well, actually, Charlie was hunting. I just went along. Ma is sure that if I have a gun I will shoot my arm off. That's because Grampa had only one arm. He got it shot off in a gun accident when he was only eight. But no matter how much I tell Ma I'm not Grampa, she still says no. Anyway, I always take some shots with Charlie's gun. He lets me, and Ma doesn't need to know.

Later

No game this morning. But in the afternoon, we did see a huge jackrabbit. It was almost as big as a raccoon. I have never seen a rabbit so big. We sure didn't have rabbits that big back in Missouri. I had the gun. When the rabbit loped across a fallen tree ahead of us, I took careful aim. And shot it.

We brought it home for supper. Ma cleaned it and cooked it up. But it made me mad to hear everyone fuss over what a big rabbit Charlie had shot. It was really me who shot it.

May 11

Charlie and me were out on Abernathy Green today. We saw Mrs. Meaney. She had a little baby propped on her hip, maybe a year old.

I couldn't help it. I burst out, "Is that your orphan child, Mrs. Meaney?"

She turned to me. "This is Henry," she said. "And he is *not* an orphan any longer."

Oh, I feel so bad! Ma and Aunt Lizzie and

me — we were all wrong to speak ill of Mrs. Meaney.

Later

Charlie and I ran home. We burst into the house and told Ma and Aunt Lizzie the news.

Aunt Lizzie was so surprised, she sat down real quick. "Well," she said, "that should be a lesson to us."

Ma didn't say anything. But after a minute, she headed off for the bedroom. She said she'd put together some baby clothes to bring to Mrs. Meaney.

Seems like we all feel bad now. Thinking ill of a good woman.

May 12

Tonight, Ma was real quiet as she went about her work. She said she was just thinking.

I asked, "On what?"

She didn't answer directly. But after a bit, she said, "Some children have no ma. No pa. Nothing. Makes you wonder."

It made me wonder if she was thinking about taking in an orphan, too. I thought of what she said that time about a sister for Becky. It made me feel guilty, thinking of a child needing a ma and pa and not having them. And thinking of that secret of Miss Emmaline's and how good she was being. So I said, "I guess, if you got a boy, it wouldn't be so bad."

Ma just burst out laughing.

Morning, May 13

I do not understand my ma. This morning, I asked why she had laughed at me.

She just laughed again. "Bring home a *boy*?" she said. "Boys are more trouble than they're worth!" But at the same time she said that, she handed me a sweet roll right out of the oven. I could see she was only teasing me. She even smiled a little.

It's the first time I've ever seen her smile in a week.

Later

Sometimes things run round and round in my head. Like this: Why would the Indians go killing people and leaving all those orphans? I know many Indians who are good. They were good to us on the trail. So why did they do what they did to the Whitmans? Maybe it's like Pa says: *Indians are like all people. Some are good. And some are not so good.*

Miss Emmaline is good. I told her that today. I said I thought Grampa would be really happy with her taking in some orphans.

Her eyes got kind of shiny and she turned away. But first she said, "I think he would, too, Josh."

May 14

Today, Charlie and I were walking in the woods. Sudden-like, two bear cubs came trundling down the hill right in front of us. We stopped talking. We stopped moving. We stopped breathing, almost. We knew the mama bear had to be nearby. If she found us near her cubs she might have us for dinner! It felt like an hour that we stood there. The cubs were long gone. But the mama never did come by. We finally went on our way. But we kept looking over our shoulders. It didn't seem right that the mama left those cubs alone. Makes me wonder if she got caught in a trap. Makes me wonder what will become of those baby bears.

Later

All I did was ask Ma if I could have a gun for my birthday.

I might as well have asked for the moon.

Ma actually swatted my behind with a broom.

Nighttime

Sometimes at night, I go off up the hill and lie on my back and look up at the sky. And I wonder about things. Like this: Does God have a reason for doing what He does? Like, for letting Grampa die? I could never ask Ma that. She'd say it was a sin to even wonder. But if Grampa were here, I could ask him. But he's not here. And it's him I want to ask God about. I also want to tell him Miss Emmaline's secret. But she's probably told him already. I wonder if he can hear us.

May 16

The sun is shining. The ground is firming up. The wind is tossing big, fluffy clouds around the sky. The women are smiling! Even Becky has stopped whining. She begged me to play the hiding game with her. I hate that game. I have to pretend not to see her, when she only hides her face. But I told her I would — later, after her nap. It seemed like a little enough thing to do.

Later. After naptime.

I told Becky I'd hide first. Sometimes, I do that and I really hide. I just go off into the woods, where I know she can't come to find me. And I read or write in my journal. But today, I just sat down behind a huge oak tree and watched her. It's what I'm doing now. She's running, looking this way and that, her hair flying every which way. The wind is blowing so hard it actually blew her over once. She just scrambled to her feet, laughing. And she's not coughing. Back in Missouri, if she ran about, she'd cough so hard she couldn't breathe. And her lips turned all blue.

Suddenly, I thought of Rachel, our little cousin who died. I remembered how she and Becky played together. Maybe missing Rachel is why Becky is so whiny. And then I thought of all those other babies who died on the trail. It almost took my breath away.

I let Becky find me.

May 17

With the dry weather, Pa says it's time to clear more trees. He and Uncle Arthur are planning a new, bigger orchard. And they plan to put in wheat, too.

We still have two oxen, which help haul out tree stumps. But after Mr. Hull got killed by a falling tree, Pa won't let me near when it's tree-felling time.

He makes me stay behind with the women. He says I can help best by helping Ma with the babies.

Makes me feel like a baby, myself. Especially because Charlie is allowed to go help.

May 20

More sunshine. Ma is smiling. Pa is humming. Charlie and I are allowed to go into the woods again. Now, if only I had a gun.

May 21

The Drucker family has come back! They are a big, noisy bunch who were with us on the trail. They left to go to California and the gold mines. But early this morning, they came back. Everybody is happy to have them. The girl, Bobbi, she was a special friend of mine. I haven't seen her since they pulled in early this morning. I'm wondering what to say when I see her. I'm feeling a bit shy. Don't exactly know why.

Midday

I needn't have worried about Bobbi. She rushed up to me, talking nonstop. Just like always. Like she'd never left at all. She says it's a big fat lie about gold in California laying about in streams. They got so poor and so hungry, they had to sell just about everything they owned to come back here and start over. And she says lots of people died out there in the gold fields. But even if the Druckers are poor, they seem happy as ever. That's their way.

So maybe Grampa was right. Maybe gold isn't worth risking your life to find.

May 22

There's plenty of work here for folks who want it. Mr. Drucker already has work in

Oregon City — for a newspaper! Half of Oregon City has emptied out, men running off to California and the mines. Pa says the Druckers are just the first to return. There will be lots more, he says.

I didn't tell him that I had been longing to go. I'm rethinking it now.

May 23

Ma and Aunt Lizzie and Miss Emmaline have decided to clean every single thing in the house. This morning, they were shaking out feather beds and hanging quilts outside almost before the sun was up. Pa took me aside. He said they meant to try and clean us up, too. So he's taking me to town today! He said he's fixing to keep me out of harm's way. What he really means is out of Ma's way — but I guess it's the same thing.

I'm so glad I have a good pa, not like Adam West's pa. Though poor Adam is dead now. He died in the flood, just like Grampa.

Later

On the way to Oregon City, Pa told me a secret: One reason we're going is for Pa to talk with Dr. McLoughlin. He's going to introduce Pa to our new governor, Joseph Lane.

I bet Ma doesn't know.

Later still

It's hot riding in the bright sunshine. Pa and me stopped to rest our horses a bit. Pa and me and the horses, we all got a good drink from a stream. Pa asked what I'd like to see when we get there. I said I don't much care. Just sitting on the bench outside the bank is excitement enough for me. And getting a chance to ride Hurricane so far is good enough, too.

Hurricane is the greatest horse ever. Grampa bought him for me. Grampa said that way I could have my own horse and come visit him when he moved to Oregon City with Miss Emmaline. Only, of course, Grampa never got to do that.

In Oregon City

Pa is in the store buying supplies. We need seed and nails and Ma wants molasses and a packet of needles. I've hitched Hurricane up at a rail.

I'm outside, watching. There are three trappers sitting on the hitching rail. One is talking to the others, like he's trying to persuade them of something. I can't understand what he's saying. They talk French with some

English words mixed in. Suddenly, they all burst out laughing. And then they all got up and went off together. But before they went, one of the men turned to me.

"*Pour vous, mon fils!*" he called out. "For you! For luck!" And he tossed me a pelt, paws and all attached! A dried and cured rabbit pelt. It is as soft as — as a rabbit!

I wonder why he gave it to me. I wonder if it will bring good luck.

Noontime

Pa and I are off to the south end of town near the falls. We are going to Dr. John McLoughlin's house. My head is still spinning from that hour in town. I saw more people in an hour than I see in a year at home. There are horses and wagons, and stores, and some of the buildings are two and three stories high! And there's a bank, and saloons, and churches. And people. Like all those trappers and even Indians walking about. I never knew there was so much out here in the world to see and to do.

At Dr. John McLoughlin's house!

Dr. McLoughlin shook hands with me like I was a grown man. I took his hand and held it firmly. But truth to tell, my heart was thunking away like crazy inside my chest. He is the biggest man I have ever seen. He is huge, maybe six and a half feet tall, almost as tall as a tree. He has a whole lot of white hair. Pa says the Indians call him White Headed Eagle. I can see why. I bet if he opened his arms wide, they'd be as broad as an eagle's wingspan.

Later

Still at Dr. McLoughlin's house.

Only thing is — this isn't really a house. It's a mansion! There's an upstairs and a downstairs, and about a hundred rooms. (Well, maybe ten or twelve.) It's painted white, and there are white curtains at the windows. I think Ma would die of happiness if she lived in a house like this.

Dr. McLoughlin said I could read any of the books I want. I think there must be a thousand books here. But Dr. McLoughlin said that Mr. Jesse Applegate of Yoncalla has the biggest library in the country. He said Mr. Applegate is called the Sage of Yoncalla.

Wait! Somebody just brought me a lemonade. More later. I surely am thirsty.

Later

Pa and Dr. McLoughlin and Mr. Joseph Lane, they were all talking together. I didn't admit I didn't know what the word "sage" meant. But I found a dictionary here and I looked it up. It's a spice, I know. But it's something else, too. It means "wise man." I feel smart for finding that out all by myself.

Nighttime, in my outside room

On the way home, Pa told me a secret. I'm about fit to bust because I can't tell it yet. But I can write it here: Pa is fixing to work with Mr. Joseph Lane, our new governor. He will help write new laws for the Oregon Territory. He'll need to have things drawn up in time for the first Territorial Legislature. It will meet here in July.

I'm so proud of my pa. I knew he was up to something like that! Pa says he can do it and still work on our homestead.

But anything new makes Ma nervous, Pa says. So we won't tell her just yet.

I have a feeling Ma knows already. Why else the squinched-up eyes? And now I have another secret that I must keep. Sometimes, I feel like I have so many secrets I will bust.

Morning, May 24

I asked Pa this morning about why Ma doesn't want him in government. For a minute, Pa was quiet. But then he said maybe there's some reason for Ma to be nervous. Like this: The Organic Act that created the Oregon Territory affirms "Utmost good will in dealing with the Indians." But our new governor, Joseph Lane, wants to hold a trial for the

Indians for the killings at the Whitman Mission. Pa says he's not sure if a trial would be a fair thing to do, or not fair. But, says Pa, he's sure of this: It will certainly lead to more bloodshed.

Later

Pa brought Ma a present back from town. It's a new apron, all blue and white checkered with long ties of lace. Ma blushed and said it made her feel like a bride. Then she went into her room, brushed her hair, and came out, her new apron tied around her. She was smiling so hard she looked like — well, like a bride.

I wanted her to keep on looking so happy. So I went and did the garden work — picked some new peas and the early lettuces and radishes for supper.

Suppertime was nice.

Nighttime

I'm lying on my bed, looking out at the stars. An owl hoots from a tree nearby. Another one answers him. A coyote cries, and it sounds like a baby crying. It's answered by another on the far hill. I imagine I hear the padding of feet — deer and elk and bears. Though, of course, they move too quietly to be heard.

I like all the excitement in Oregon City. I can never wait to get there. But after we're there a while, I can't wait to get back home.

I think I'm beginning to love the mountains.

Early morning, May 25

I have wrapped the rabbit pelt around my diary as a new cover. It's soft and feels good in my hands. I wonder if it will really bring good luck.

I'm thinking about what Pa said about Indians and laws. Pa said the Indians have their own laws. And white people have their own laws. And they're different, sometimes real different. So how can white people's laws work for Indians? Pa says he doesn't think they can. And the laws of the Indians don't work for white people. So how could a trial settle anything? That, says Pa, is called a dilemma.

More later. Ma is hollering for me. She doesn't sound happy.

Later

I forgot to close the gate after me in the garden last night. And deer or rabbits or hedgehogs — or maybe all of them — got in overnight. They ate every one of Ma's vegetables, snap beans, new carrots, and tiny shoots of corn. The whole garden is just gnawed away. What's left is bent and trampled. "Now," said Ma, "I must do work that I have already done." She didn't even sound mad. Just sad. And that made me feel terrible.

I spent the whole day helping her plant another garden. Miss Emmaline worked right alongside us. She strung more wire around the bottom of the fence so creatures couldn't burrow under. She took me aside and said not to worry. The sunshine will work fast on the little seedlings, she said.

I hope she's right.

May 26

Today I put Hector in the back sling Pa made for him. I took him down by the river. If you keep him moving, it keeps him quiet. He really is a sweet little baby, all fat with round cheeks and the biggest eyes you ever did see. If he'd only stop yelling he'd be much more fun to have around.

I'm still trying to make up to Ma. I hate to see her sad. Specially after she was so happy the night before.

May 30

Every evening, I look to see if the sun has done its work on the garden. I think it's beginning to. Already there are lots of tiny green shoots coming up. There are weeds shooting up between the rows. I pick them out carefully, giving the plants every chance to get the sun. And afterwards, I'm always sure to shut the gate tight behind me when I leave.

June 2

It must be working — or something's working. Ma said tonight that it's good to see me acting responsibly.

I had to turn my back, I was smiling so hard. I felt so good inside me, where no one could see but me.

Nighttime

Tonight, Pa was up late reading and making notes on his tablet by candlelight. I couldn't sleep none, so I got up and joined him at the table. We sat together, not speaking. Just reading and being kind of friendly-quiet together. After a bit, Pa looked up at me. "Do you miss schooling, Josh?" he asked.

I nodded. "A lot," I said.

"There's a school in Oregon City," Pa said.

"I know," I said.

I didn't say more. I just waited, my heart thundering hard.

But Pa didn't say more, either. He just went back to his book. I know Pa. He's thinking about school for me. I'm so excited. Maybe the rabbit pelt is bringing me luck. Just imagine: school. Oregon City. That's adventure enough.

June 3

Tonight, Ma said she wants to go to Oregon City. Aunt Lizzie and Uncle Arthur and Miss Emmaline want to go, too. I know why. That new apron made Ma think about all she was missing, with stores and pretty things in town. I know, too, that Pa has a little gold to spend from some trading he did in town last week.

I offered to care for Becky and Hector when they went.

Ma just widened her eyes at me. I know she was surprised I'd offer. Aunt Lizzie said, "Why not? He watches Becky plenty of times."

Ma said she'd think about it.

I don't really want to watch Becky and Hector. But I need to show more of that "responsibility."

My birthday's in nearly two weeks.

June 4

This afternoon they'll go to town — Ma and Pa and Aunt Lizzie and Uncle Arthur and Miss Emmaline. Aunt Lizzie is taking little Isabel with her. Charlie's staying with me. Both of our mas and our pas said there should be two of us with Hector and Becky.

Charlie wanted to go to town so bad. We were out on the porch, and he kicked the door, really hard. Luckily, Aunt Lizzie was already back in the house, so she didn't see. But maybe she heard because she called over her shoulder, "And you'd better have the garden weeded by the time we get back."

Then Charlie kicked a chair. He kicked it so hard, it flew across the porch.

It's going to be a long six hours with a fussing baby and a whining Becky. And Charlie kicking doors and chairs every which way.

Afternoon

They've left. Hector's napping. Becky begs to go into the woods. She begs to play house. She begs to play horsey. She begs for hide-and-seek.

I just want to write in my diary and read Grampa's poetry book. I said when Hector wakes up, I'll put him in his sling. And we'll all walk along the path by the river. As long as it's light, we don't have to worry about bears and wolves.

Becky squealed and clapped her hands. She said she can't wait to see a bear. Now she's digging in the dirt under the almond tree. I don't see Charlie anywhere. He's not weeding the garden, that's for sure. I bet he went off to fish by himself. And he didn't even tell me. It's not my fault that his ma and pa made him stay here.

Need to check on Hector.

Later

He's still sleeping. He looks sweet — all warm, his cheeks pink and round, his fist curled up on the pillow. At least when he sleeps he doesn't yell.

Becky's under the tree. She's talking quietly

to her baby doll. She named her doll Pudding Head. I asked her why once. She shrugged. Then she said, "And her middle name is Pumpkin."

She just asked again when we were going to see the bears. I told her we weren't going to see bears, just deer maybe, and we'd go as soon as Hector wakes up and for heaven's sake be patient.

She stuck her lip out at me.

Later

I went to get Grampa's poetry book. Sometimes, when I read it, I want to write my own poems. But I could never be a poet. Maybe I'll just be like Pa and write laws some day.

Now what? Becky's gone from under the tree.

"Becky?"

No answer.

Hiding. Playing her dumb old game. But I guess I have to go look for her.

Later. Much later.

I've looked all over. Where is she? She makes me so mad. Maybe she went looking for Charlie.

At the river

Charlie was fishing there. But he hadn't seen Becky. And, he said, he's going farther upstream where the trout are bigger.

I said, "Thanks a lot."

He said, "You're welcome."

Sometimes I think Charlie's as much of a baby as Becky.

Back at the house

I called. I looked. I called some more.

She won't answer.

I know she's hiding. When she finally comes out, I'm going to give her bottom a good hard swat.

Now Hector's howling. I changed his diaper and he grinned up at me. He wriggled and tried to flip over. He can't do that trick yet, though, so I helped. He got on all fours then and tried to scoot away from me. I scooped him back.

All I have to do is wait here. Becky will give up. I'm not calling her even one more time.

Hector is trying to stick his finger in my mouth. I can't help smiling at him. But I am worried.

A little bit.

A lot.

An hour later

I have looked everywhere. Everywhere but the woods. I even thought maybe she fell asleep somewhere in the house. But she's nowhere.

There's a little clock on the mantel. She's been gone almost an hour. My heart is thundering in my chest. On the trail, if a child was gone for an hour, she was lost for good. Or dead.

But we're not on the trail. We're in Oregon. In a house. In the Willamette Valley.

Here, being gone does not mean being dead.

Please, God.

I'll get the sling for my back and put Hector in it. Then, go find Charlie.

Please, God, don't let her go to the woods.

And if she did go there, God, don't let a bear find her first.

A few minutes later

I found Charlie. I told him Becky's still missing. He's scared, too. He wants to go with me. I said no. He should get some neighbors. The Hulls are the closest. They'll help organize a search. And someone has to be here in case Becky comes back.

Charlie said to leave Hector with him. But when I went to hand him over, Hector almost flung himself out of Charlie's arms, screaming and reaching for me. I took him back and he stopped howling. I put him on my back in the sling again. I picked up Charlie's gun then. I didn't even ask. I just said that I'd shoot it off if . . . I mean, *when* . . . I find her.

Outside

I hurried down the animal trail that leads into the forest, Hector bouncing against my back. I figured Becky would follow the trail. She wouldn't just bust through the underbrush.

I looked for footprints. None. Just deer backs. And the trail of a lynx. Lynx don't bother you. They shy away. I talked to Hector to keep up my own courage.

He gurgled at me.

I found something then — a bit of something clinging to a branch. Becky's dress? I held it up to the little bit of light that filtered between the leaves. No. Just fluff, something a bird dropped while making a nest.

The rifle was heavy. Hector was heavy. I stopped for a minute to rest, then went on, hurrying. It was getting darker. Soon I'd reach the water hole.

The animals come there at dusk. Becky would come, too, if she followed the trail.

There were deer there already, a mama and a still-speckled fawn.

No bears.

No wolves.

No Becky.

Dark now, almost

It came to me then. Stop still. Be like the Indians. The trappers. Listen.

I did. Scurrying in the underbrush. A rabbit. Squirrels. Wind brushing the leaves.

Nothing else.

"Becky?" I called.

Listened.

An echo came back. *Becky . . . Becky . . . Becky?*

A jay scolded. A crow flew overhead. The crow was laughing.

Tears started up to my eyes.

Don't cry. Only babies cry.

Not true. I'd seen Pa cry. When Rachel died. When Grampa died.

Nobody's dead.

Much later

I don't know how far I went. Hector was fussing by then. It was getting really dark the farther in I walked. And then I heard something — a rumbling sound. A thudding.

I stopped. What was it? Something heavy. Thunder maybe? A storm building up? No.

Quiet again. The only sound was Hector. I could tell he was working up to a real howl. I reached around and patted him. Soon. We'd go home soon, I told him. Maybe Becky was already there waiting for us.

Should I turn back now?

Above me, a woodpecker made his rat-tat sound. And . . . something else. That sound again. Thuddy sound. Underbrush crashing.

A bear? Please no.

"Becky?" I called softly. And then I shouted. "Becky!"

No more thudding. Everything still. She wouldn't be hiding still — would she?

It *was* something different I'd heard, wasn't it? I kept standing there, my head tilted. Hector began to fuss louder, pounding his little fists against my back.

"Stop it!" I told him. "Hush!"

And then — yes! A shot! Someone shot off a rifle. A signal? About Becky? Or just a hunter?

Below was a ravine, thick with underbrush.

The shot came from below. I hurtled toward the sound, clawing my way down the ravine. Slipping. Sliding, the rifle banging against my leg. I held back branches that snatched at my face, holding them away from Hector.

More sounds. Close by. A clunk. A thud. Someone reloading.

Another shot.

I lost my footing, then scrambled back to my feet, fighting my way toward the sound.

Hector was flailing around, howling, his head wobbly against my back.

"Hold on," I cried. "Hold on. Just one more minute. We're going to find Becky."

We did.

Later

A trapper had found her first. She was sitting on a log. A thin, dirty mountain man sat beside her, his rifle in one hand, his other patting Becky's muddy hair. She was soaking wet, her dress torn and filthy. Her face was streaked with tears and dirt. There was a long red gash down one cheek. But she was there. Alive. Whole.

And on the ground behind her was the biggest, blackest, deadest bear I have ever seen.

"Where were you?!" Becky cried when she saw me. She stood up and reached for me.

Where was *I*?

I reached for her.

Later still

I was so happy, tears were running down my face. I was so mad I wanted nothing more than to swat her. And I was so scared I didn't even dare look toward the bear again.

The feelings fought with one another. Mad won out. But I didn't swat her.

I just grabbed her shoulders. "Why did you run off?" I said.

"I didn't," she said.

"You did, too!" I said.

And then . . . we hugged.

Hector stopped howling. He kicked against my back.

And I began to breathe again.

"Zee bear," the trapper muttered.

I turned to him.

"Theeze gurl?" he said, pointing at Becky. Then he pointed behind him at the bear, shaking his head. "Ooh, ooh! Like zee devil."

He moved his feet rapidly, up and down, up and down, stamping hard. Then he pounded his rifle butt on the ground, three, four times, as though to make the thudding sound of a bear running. "Boom! Boom!" he said.

He grinned at me then. His teeth were stained brown and all crookedy. But I suddenly thought it the sweetest smile I had ever seen.

I could only stare at him. And then I looked at the bear, all stretched out and dead, its mouth open, yellow saliva dripping, its teeth curved and brown and snarly looking. I looked at Becky and swallowed down tears that rushed up my throat.

She reached for my hand. "Let's go home?" she said.

At home

I'm in my lean-to. A candle's by my side. I think my heart has only just now begun to slow. I have never been so scared. I was more scared today than even the time I got lost on the trail. And I was plenty scared then.

Ma and Pa and the neighbors, the Hulls

and Druckers and . . . well, I'm too tired to write about it now. I've already written in the entries above, ones I couldn't write in the woods. (Grampa said record it all.) But I have to write one thing more before I sleep: I know Ma is going to be real mad at me tomorrow — after she gets over being so happy. And I can tell that Pa is deep disappointed in me for losing Becky — even though I did find her again. But I also know this: I am the luckiest child God ever made.

June 5

Today, I had to tell it all again. And again. Becky told it again, too. Only thing is, every time Becky told the story, it changed. About the only true part of her story is this: She decided to take "just a little walk" in the woods. She saw a bear, and a man shot and killed the bear. By the time she told it for the tenth time, though, the man was an Indian with feathers. And she had patted the bear.

June 6

This is the real story. I'm not sure of the details, because the trapper spoke mostly French, just a word or two of English mixed in. But with a mix of sign language and such, this is the story I got: He heard crying in the woods. He followed the sound. He found Becky. At the same time, a huge she-bear found her. It came barreling down the hill toward her. The rest of the story was grunts and waves and grinning — but I figure that he shot the bear once through the lungs. And the second shot was just to make sure.

I figure now that maybe I am not the luckiest child alive. Maybe Becky is.

June 7

I keep waiting for Ma to start in scolding me. She doesn't. Instead, every time I walk by her, she just grabs me and holds me to her. Not a word. Just holds on to me, like she's holding on for dear life.

But Pa is deep disappointed in me, I think. I see him frowning at me, like he's trying to figure something out. Maybe he's wondering how come I could be so careless. I always look away when he's studying me like that.

June 8

I'm feeling real guilty for being so careless. I didn't mean to be. I just looked away for a few minutes. But I know that's no excuse. A few minutes, and my baby sister could be dead.

I will never let her out of my sight again. I wonder now if this is how Ma feels.

June 9

Ma and Aunt Lizzie and Miss Emmaline have been cooking and baking up a feast. Everybody is invited to come tomorrow. The Gibbons and the Hulls and the Wests and Mr. and Mrs. Meaney — who will bring Henry, their new child — and the Druckers and everybody. They are all invited.

Everybody swarmed into the woods, searching for Becky when Charlie went running to them. And then, after Becky was found, they all stayed to hug and celebrate. Ma is repaying their kindness with food. It's the way she knows best.

June 10

The party has gone on for the whole day. There is singing and food and folks talking and laughing. There's dancing, just like at the beginning of the trail. The Druckers came from Kentucky, and they showed the women how to do a jig. Ma and Aunt Lizzie got up on the porch with Bobbi and Ma Drucker, dancing and laughing as though they was all Bobbi's age. Mr. Drucker played the fiddle. And the Hull children amused themselves by clambering up every tree in sight, like little monkeys. Miss Emmaline has Hector in one arm, Baby Isabel in the other, and about a dozen other children clambering up her skirts. Ma has tables spread with more meats and pies and jams than I have maybe ever seen. All the ladies brought something. Even Miss Emmaline baked a whole mincemeat pie by herself. And didn't burn it, either.

Later

One thing wrong: Becky is acting too big for her britches. She tells her bear story over and over again. And each time it gets more wild. Bigger and bigger lies. Her last story was that a huge Indian found her, picked her up, and gave her a ride on the back of a bear. And she tickled the bear under its chin.

I told her to stop telling lies.

Ma said to leave her be.

Later, at the party

Everybody is fussing over Becky, thanking God over and over that she's home safe. They seem to notice me as only an afterthought. All they ask about is the trapper and why he just disappeared into the woods again. I feel like saying: Well, if it wasn't for me, there wouldn't be a party today. But then I think: And if it wasn't for me, Becky wouldn't have gotten lost in the first place.

I guess I had best keep my mouth shut.

Nighttime

Almost dark now. Folks just beginning to drift off toward home. Before they left, Pa called everyone to be still and quiet a while. And he offered up the prettiest, thankfullest prayer. You just knew it came right from his heart. He asked God's blessing on his children. He thanked God for sparing Becky. And he thanked God for me — me for being so brave!

Ma had tears in her eyes.

I think most folks did.

I know I did.

Maybe Pa isn't too mad at me after all.

Nighttime

Just a thin slice of moon above, looking in on my bed. I feel so happy about Becky, even if she is a bother. And happy that Ma isn't mad. But I worry about Pa.

He did say in the prayer that I was brave. But even so, I do believe he is disappointed in me. He is so silent. And he keeps looking hard at me. I don't think Pa has ever said a harsh word to me. I think I deserve to hear many harsh words.

Morning, June 11

Oh, I am so happy I could shout. Or sing. Or — something! Pa is not angry at me. Not at all. I asked. I had to face up to him. Pa says anyone can be distracted for a moment. Children get lost. Look at what happened on the trail, he said, all those babies who died. Then he said that I showed real courage and brains when I went after Becky. And he talked about all the other good, brave, and strong things I have done since I was just nine years old.

It was a long, long list.

I was so pleased. I could feel myself blushing just like a girl.

Later

Another thing. I asked Pa why he keeps looking hard at me. He laughed. He says I've shot up so tall, he thinks sometimes he's seeing another man in the house.

June 13

Ma has a bit of mirror hanging on the wall in the kitchen. I don't often look in it. But today I climbed on a chair to try and see my whole self. And Pa is right. I am shooting up. My pants come up almost to my shins. Ma caught me on the chair, looking at myself. She says she'll make some new pants for me soon. Now that I've gotten too big for my britches, she said. But she said it smiling.

June 15

Pa and Ma have a secret from me. They stop talking as soon as I come in a room. But I can tell it's a happy secret.

I don't ask. But I think I know. It's about my birthday present. I believe it will be a gun. Now that I'm almost a man.

June 16

At supper tonight, Miss Emmaline looked at me and smiled, a little secret smile. Then she took a deep breath and pushed her chair back a little from the table, turning to face Pa and Uncle Arthur.

"I've picked out a home site," she said. "I can build a house myself. But I'd like a little help framing it up."

For a minute, nobody spoke, just stared bug-eyed at her.

And then, like it was the most ordinary thing in the world, she added, "And I mean to adopt a baby. Two babies, actually."

I have to say I found myself grinning then — and not just at the look on everybody's faces. I was smiling because Miss Emmaline was smiling so big. I haven't seen her look that happy since the day she and Grampa got married.

Still no one said a word. It was like everyone was bewitched. Then Miss Emmaline got up and started clearing the table. "I'll need help," she said softly, turning slightly toward Ma and Aunt Lizzie, kind of shy looking. "I know nothing about babies. And not much about cooking. I guess I'm better with a hammer than I am with a stove."

At that, everyone burst out laughing. And that seemed to break the spell. Ma got to her feet. Aunt Lizzie got up, too. All three of them began hugging and hugging, and laughing and hugging, rocking back and forth. And then — well, then they did what women always do when they're happy. They cried.

That didn't worry me none. I'm used to it by now.

Later

After that was over, Ma turned back to Pa and Charlie and Uncle Arthur and me. She was grinning so wide, the smile almost split her face.

"That," said Ma, "is the best plan I have heard since . . ."

She stopped and looked directly at Pa. And then she said softly, "Since Mr. McCullough here suggested we come to Oregon."

June 22. My birthday!

No! It's better than a gun. It's far, far better, though I got a gun, too, a really good one to bring home game, not just a birding rifle. I will need it, riding those long, long ways on Hurricane to Oregon City.

Because yes — Pa has arranged that I will

go to school! I will study at Dr. McLoughlin's school. I will study with Mr. Applegate.

My head is spinning. I will ride off each day to Oregon City. I may even board in town come winter.

I can tell Ma is worried. Still, she says I can do it.

I can hardly stop smiling.

August now

July has spun past us, and so much has happened. Pa spent much of July working at the first congress, writing up laws and such. Ma still frowns when he talks about that. But I think she's getting used to new things.

Miss Emmaline's little house is finished. Pa and me and Charlie and Uncle Arthur and Miss Emmaline, we worked all summer getting it just right. Ma made curtains and everybody brought some things for setting up house. It was like Miss Emmaline was a bride again. She'll be moving over in about a week. And after that, she will be bringing home two orphans. They are brother and sister, Melinda and Chester, four and five years old. Becky can't wait. I know why. She will spend her whole time bossing them around. But maybe that's all right, too. And I think Miss Emmaline will make a just fine mother.

I think Grampa would be very, very happy.

September now

Summer is waning and mist and damp sets in at night. Smoke from chimneys fills the sky.

I start my schooling next week. I'm so excited, so happy.

One thing bad: I'm going to miss Charlie something awful. He has no wish to go with me to school.

I wonder what he'll do all day without me. He says he'll miss me lots.

Nighttime, in my little outdoor room

I'm lying on my bed, the moonlight slipping through the open shutters. It's late, really, really late, but I'm not able to sleep. Tomorrow I ride off to Oregon City. My first time alone.

At suppertime, Becky asked was I scared. I said no. That's not true. I am scared, a little. But I've been scared half to death all of this past wild year and look what I've done.

Sleep won't come, so I got up and stood looking out over the fields, the valley, the orchard shooting up, trees weaving shadows in the moonlight. And I thought of all we've done this past wild year: crossing prairies and mountains and rivers, building a house, planting orchards and gardens. And Pa helping to create a government.

And then I think of tomorrow, and I feel like morning will never come. Because now comes the biggest adventure of my life, the most exciting thing that has happened to me since — well, since Pa first said, "Let's set out for Oregon."

Life in America
in 1849

Historical Note

In August 1848, President James Polk signed the Oregon Territorial Organic Act, creating the Territory of Oregon. By that time, Oregon was experiencing the immigration of thousands upon thousands of settlers who had arrived at the end of the Oregon Trail.

President James K. Polk.

These adventurers had left their homes in the East to look for money, adventure, open spaces, and, in some cases, a healthier environment.

The Oregon Trail.

But once the early settlers reached Oregon, at the end of that long and perilous trail, their struggles weren't over. There were many more obstacles to overcome: lack of food, sickness, seemingly constant rain, floods, Native American threats, and the ever present dangers of wild animals.

One particular difficulty, which few could have envisioned, came from the lack of laws governing the territory. Also, the Hudson's Bay Fur Company, which owned the sole rights to the

Hudson's Bay Fur Company's trading post.

fur trade in the territory, did not want settlers there, so there was constant friction between the settlers and the company that had dominated the territory for so long.

But the settlers were a tough bunch, and in spite of the difficulties, they did their best to prosper and overcome.

Hudson's Bay Fur Company's trading store.

Some, however, decided to move on — the Gold Rush was well underway by then, and visions, often mistaken, of instant gold were hard to ignore. But the ones who stayed found a true friend in Dr. John McLoughlin, an employee of Hudson's Bay Fur Company, who also served as mayor of Oregon City. Dr. McLoughlin was a wise and strong man whose word was law in the territory. But he was also a compassionate, caring man who helped many settlers survive their first winter — a winter made difficult because they were often poor, exhausted by the trip, and had wagons and animals so worn out that they were of little use to them. His kindness involved lending money and providing boats and food to the settlers, as well as many other, less tangible things — such as hope. He also set up the first school in Oregon City, one that was a boon to the early settlers.

Dr. John McLoughlin.

But there was trouble on the way. The trouble came in the form of retaliation for the attack on the Whitman Mission. Joseph Lane, the new governor of Oregon who took office in March 1849, was intent on bringing to justice the members of the Cayuse tribe who had taken part in the Whitmans' massacre. Years earlier, the Whitmans had set up a mission to care for the Native

Christian missionaries preaching to Native Americans.

Americans. But when an epidemic of measles broke out and many Native Americans died, they believed that Dr. Whitman had caused the disaster. And so, in November 1847, the Native Americans attacked the Mission, killing the Whitmans and many other men and women, leaving behind dozens of orphaned children. But could there be any real justice when Native Americans' laws and white men's laws came into conflict? It was one of the many things that had to be settled by the new government.

An early Oregon settlement.

For the early settlers, these struggles were part of the price they were willing to pay at the end of their incredible journey — the price of a new adventure, a new land. A new place to call home.

About the Author

When Patricia Hermes first began the series about Joshua and the Oregon Trail, she knew — through her own experiences moving to new places — how hard it must have been for Joshua to leave family and friends and journey across that lonesome prairie. As she continued to write about him, and to see him through two books, Joshua began to seem as though he were living and breathing within the pages of the book. He experienced great losses. He coped with terrible tragedies and the death of someone whom he loved dearly. And he found great joys along the way, as he and his family made Oregon their home in a nearly "perfect place." And now, in this last book about Joshua, he experiences even more daring adventures and more excitement as he begins to grow into manhood — and finds his way through a very "wild year."

Patricia Hermes is the author of more than thirty books for children and young adults. She has written five other books for the My America series: *Our Strange New Land*, *The Starving Time*, and *Season of Promise*, which are the stories of Elizabeth Barker's experiences in the Jamestown Colony in 1609, as well as Joshua's first two diaries, *Westward to Home* and *A Perfect Place*. Many of her books have received awards, from Children's Choice awards to state awards, and also ALA Best Books and ALA Notable Book awards.

For Michael Paul Nastu

Acknowledgments

Grateful acknowledgment is made for permission to reprint the following:

Cover Portrait by Glenn Harrington

Page 99 (top): President James K. Polk, Library of Congress, via Scholastic Online Digital Archive.

Page 99 (bottom): Map of the Oregon Trail, Getty Images, New York.

Page 100: Hudson's Bay Fur Company trading post, North Wind Pictures, Alfred, Maine.

Page 101: Hudson's Bay Fur Company store, North Wind Pictures, Alfred, Maine.

Page 102: Dr. John McLoughlin, Courtesy of the McLoughlin Memorial Association, Oregon City, Oregon.

Page 103: Missionaries preaching, Culver Pictures, New York.

Page 104: Early Oregon settlement, Culver Pictures, New York.

Other books in the My America series

While the events described and some of the characters in this book may be based on actual historical events and real people, Joshua McCullough is a fictional character, created by the author, and his diary is a work of fiction.

Library of Congress Cataloging-in-Publication Data
Hermes, Patricia.
The wild year : Joshua's Oregon Trail diary / by Patricia Hermes.
    p.   cm. — (My America ; bk. 3)
ISBN 0-439-37055-8; 0-439-37056-6 (pbk.)
2002044576
CIP AC

10 9 8 7 6 5 4 3 2 1   03 04 05 06 07

The display type was set in Cooper Old Style.
The text type was set in Goudy.
Book design by Elizabeth Parisi
Photo research by Amla Sanghvi

Printed in the U.S.A.   23
First edition, August 2003